KING OF THE CASTLE

KING OF THE CASTLE

by

Kathy Stinson

illustrated by Kasia Charko

SECOND STORY *Press*

CANADIAN CATALOGUING IN PUBLICATION DATA

Stinson, Kathy
King of the castle

ISBN 1-896764-35-5

I. Charko, Kasia, 1949-   . II. Title.

PS8587.T56K56 2000   jC813'.54   C00-932103-9
PZ7.S74Ki 2000

Edited by Shaun Oakey
Design by Emily Schultz

Second Story Press gratefully acknowledges the assistance of the Ontario Arts
Council and the Canada Council for the Arts for our publishing program.
We acknowledge the financial support of the Government of Canada
through the Book Publishing Industry Development Program
for our publishing activities.

Printed and bound in Canada

Published by
SECOND STORY PRESS
720 Bathurst Street, Suite 301
Toronto Canada M5S 2R4

Dedicated to Elijah Allen,
whose story inspired me

CHAPTER ONE

$\mathcal{M}$R. ELLIOT LIKED being a caretaker. Every day he hoisted the flag in front of Jessie Lucas Public School as proud as could be. He pushed his broom through classrooms and hallways, gathering paper scraps, stray erasers and schoolyard dirt. The clean smell of sawdust and lemons followed wherever he swept.

To a boy standing outside the principal's office looking like he was probably in trouble, Mr. Elliot said, "Good morning, Derek." To a student in the library bent over her paper, he said, "You're working hard, Sal."

"I have to write the capital cities of a bunch of countries on my map." Sal pointed to her atlas. "I'm not sure which of these cities is the capital of Canada."

"Hmm," Mr. Elliot said. "Nice job of colouring your map you've done there."

He pushed his broom into the hall and past a group of kids painting a mural full of things that live in a pond. "You'll wipe up any spills, eh, fellas?"

At coffee break, someone knocked on the door of the caretakers' room. "Mr. Elliot," Mario said, "could you come and get our ball down off the roof?"

"Sure thing." Mr. Elliot poured the rest of his coffee down the sink. He followed Mario and his friends out to the playground with his ladder.

"Up there." Mario pointed to the roof of the library.

There was a nip in the fall air but sun enough to keep it from being too sharp. Up on the roof Mr. Elliot felt like singing, *I'm the king of the castle and you're the dirty rascal.*

Mr. Elliot didn't always feel so much like King of the Castle.

All kinds of balls dotted the gravel-covered roof — tennis balls, a hackey sack, a volleyball, a soccer ball. The rubber balls bounced as Mr. Elliot threw them down to the ground.

"Can you play soccer with us now, Mr. Elliot?" one of the kids asked.

Mr. Elliot dribbled the ball out to the field and around one player after another, until Derek snuck in from the side and gave the ball a walloping kick.

The ball sailed over the fence into a backyard.

"Way to go, Derek!" Mario shouted.

"I'll get it." Mr. Elliot jogged to the fence. "People don't yell at grownups like they do kids."

"But Mr. Elliot!" the kids shouted as he scrambled over the fence. "The sign!"

From behind a garage leaped a large black dog, barking and showing its sharp teeth. Mr. Elliot grabbed the ball and hurled it back to the playground. He made it to the fence just as the dog got hold of his pant leg. A man stormed out of the house. "Idiot! Can't you read?!"

Mr. Elliot pulled himself free of the dog's teeth but left a scrap of brown caretaker pants behind.

He jumped down from the fence into the school-yard.

Derek hollered back at the neighbour, "*You're* an idiot. Of course he can read."

"Don't be rude," Mr. Elliot said. He tucked his shirt back into his torn pants and returned to the caretakers' room with his ladder.

CHAPTER TWO

EVEN MORE THAN being a caretaker, Mr. Elliot liked being a grandfather. He played net whenever Jason wanted to practise his shots on goal and made music for Jemma on his harmonica.

Ever since Jemma was a baby, Mr. Elliot played his music and sang to her at bedtime. "Hush, little baby, don't say a word . . ." Jemma loved this song even though she wasn't a baby anymore, but one night when her grandfather was singing it to her, she slipped off her bed and brought him a book. "Read to me, Grampa," she said.

Mr. Elliot kept on singing, "Mama's going to buy you . . ."

"Stop singing," Jemma insisted. "Read."

"I'll have to let your mother read you your book," Mr. Elliot said, "because I don't have my glasses."

He turned away from Jemma's big brown eyes, ashamed of telling her a lie.

Oh, why did Jemma have to bother him with her book anyway? Jason had never asked him to read. Neither had his own daughter when she was little.

After Jason and Jemma had gone to bed Mr. Elliot's daughter said, "Is something bothering you, Dad?"

"Not really." Mr. Elliot banged his coffee mug down on the counter harder than he'd meant to.

CHAPTER THREE

$\mathcal{T}$HE NEXT DAY at school a Kindergarten student stopped Mr. Elliot in the hall. "Can you tell me which of these papers is for the principal and which is for the nurse?" she asked. "My teacher told me but I forgot."

"Sorry, Naomi, my glasses are broken. I can't see what the papers say."

If I could read, Mr. Elliot thought, I could stop telling so many lies.

Mr. Elliot pushed his broom around the corner past more classrooms. In Grade One, the kids were singing a song about autumn leaves. The kids in Grade Two were busy writing. Someone in Grade Three was giving a speech. The Grade Four teacher was reading a story to his class. Their laughter drifted into the hallway.

Mr. Elliot stopped sweeping for a moment. He fiddled with a sticker one of the kids had stuck to his broom as the teacher continued to read. "My nose's name is Norbert. No, that's not right. Norbert lives in my nose. He's from Jupiter originally but, for the past little while, he's been staying with me." And the kids in Grade Four laughed some more.

If I could read, Mr. Elliot thought, I could read to Jemma and Jason, and make them laugh.

At coffee break Mr. Elliot went to the caretakers' room. Mr. Caracas was writing up an order from the supply catalogue. "I've been thinking," he said. "You know I'm retiring next year."

"We'll miss you here." Mr. Elliot tucked his broom behind the door.

"I think you should apply for my job." Mr. Caracas handed Mr. Elliot a form. "You'd make a fine head custodian."

"Thanks." Mr. Elliot knew that to do Mr. Caracas's job — to order equipment and supplies from the catalogue and make up work schedules for all the caretakers in the neighbourhood — he could not get away with just pretending to be able to read. But he looked at the paper Mr. Caracas had given him anyway, until Mr. Caracas left the room.

If I could read, Mr. Elliot thought, I could stop pretending all the time that I can.

Mr. Elliot tucked the paper into his mail cubby where he kept his supply of chocolate chip cookies.

Then he kicked an empty bucket into the corner.

CHAPTER FOUR

THE ROOMS MR. ELLIOT swept after school that day seemed more jam-packed full of words than ever. Words on the walls and on charts and on the children's desks. Words that so many children — even the littlest ones — were learning to read.

Mr. Elliot was dusting the shelves in the library when he heard laughter in the hallway. But it wasn't a happy sound like when the kids were listening to their story.

"We can't have Derek in our group," someone yelled. "We'll get the lowest mark for sure."

"Did you see when the teacher asked him to read today?" another student said. "He didn't even know what page we were on."

Again everyone laughed.

Mr. Elliot's cheeks burned and his stomach

tightened in a knot. He went to the doorway with his broom. Several kids were standing together. Derek, standing alone, yanked his jacket from the hook.

"Give me a hand in here, Derek, would you?" Mr. Elliot said.

Derek scowled. The other kids drifted off down the hall.

"Can you lift the other end of this table for me?" Mr. Elliot said.

Derek took his end. "Where to?"

"Um, just over there beside the bathtub."

Derek helped Mr. Elliot move the table.

"Looks dumb here," Derek said.

"You're right. Let's move it back." They set the table down back where it was before. "Don't let them get to you, Derek, okay?"

"I hate being the stupid one," Derek said. "Makes me want to smash someone."

"I know," Mr. Elliot said. "But don't give up on your schoolwork, okay? You can do it."

Derek shrugged. "Anything else?"

"Not today. Thanks."

Mr. Elliot finished dusting the shelves. He pushed his broom down the hall, thinking, Who do you think you are, Graham Elliot, telling Derek, 'Don't give up, you can do it'? You are a coward to say such things when you cannot read yourself.

He flung his broom into the closet of the caretakers' room.

$\mathcal{M}$R. ELLIOT UNLOCKED his bike from the rack. He pedalled along the tree-lined street. It had been a hard day. Worst was hearing the kids laughing at Derek. It brought back too many memories of when he was a boy — how he always forgot the sounds of the letters on the board, how the words on the page somehow flopped around so they didn't make sense. He remembered the feel of the teacher's ruler across his knuckles when the letters he tried to print would not go on the lines he was trying so hard to put them on. When those kids were laughing at Derek today, it was like the kids at Sycamore School laughing at him all over again.

Up ahead, a lone figure ambled along the side of the road. His jeans hung low on his hips, his plaid flannel shirt-jacket was long, and his black

baseball cap was on backwards. He kicked a stone from the end of a driveway. It tumbled along the pavement and into the gutter in front of the next house. The boy kicked it again each time he caught up with it.

As Mr. Elliot got close enough to recognize him, Derek picked up the stone and hurled it at a red hexagonal sign with white letters. It made a satisfying clang against the metal, and a dent too, Mr. Elliot saw when he got to the corner.

"Throw one for me too, Derek, would you?"

"What?" Derek looked up at the caretaker, surprised.

"Nothing," Mr. Elliot said. "Keep your nose clean, eh?" There you go again, he thought, giving out advice you've got no business giving. He turned the corner and pedalled home.

That night Mr. Elliot fixed Jason's reading light and played a tune on his harmonica for Jemma. Before he started to sing her a lullaby, Jemma came to him with her book.

"Not tonight, Jemma," he said quietly. He turned away so Jemma wouldn't see how much he was hurting.

While his daughter read Jason and Jemma their bedtime stories, Mr. Elliot sat in the kitchen and drank another cup of coffee.

"I wonder," he said, when his daughter came back from tucking in his grandchildren. "I've been wondering . . ." He took a long time to swallow the last mouthful of his coffee. Finally he said, "I want to learn to read."

"You? Now?"

"I know, I'm old. Right? A grandfather!"

"Well, yes."

"And a grandfather should be able to read stories to his grandchildren," Mr. Elliot declared. "I want to try to learn."

"I'll make some calls tomorrow," Mr. Elliot's daughter said.

CHAPTER SIX

$\mathcal{T}$HE DAY MR. ELLIOT was to start his reading lessons, he thought the butterflies pounding around in his stomach must be wearing soccer shoes — with cleats! He was so nervous he almost changed his mind about going.

What if I look stupid? he thought. What if I *am* stupid? What if I make a fool of myself?

At the end of the day Mr. Elliot leaned his broom in the closet. He would not tell anyone at school about the lessons. What if things just didn't work out?

In the hall little Naomi asked, "Are your glasses fixed yet?"

Mr. Elliot shook his head. He rode his bike through crunchy leaves, down the street, past two traffic lights, then up the big hill to the public library.

His daughter had told him, "Watch for the building with the big rabbit and turtle beside the doors." And there it was.

Mr. Elliot soon found himself in a room with four other people, all adults, who looked just as scared as he felt. Mr. Elliot's heart thumped. Could he really put himself through all this again? The struggling over letters and words? The humiliation of getting them wrong?

Mr. Elliot sat on the edge of his chair squeezing his hands between his knees, hoping the teacher would not ask him any questions, or worse, ask him to read.

"Good afternoon, everyone," a dark-haired woman said. "My name is Brenda. I'm going to be your teacher."

After the students introduced themselves, the teacher showed them how to write the words *I can*. Everyone copied the words on the first page of their notebooks. They wrote *I can* three times. Then the teacher asked each of the students how

they would finish an *I can* sentence. She wrote down the words for each sentence on a chart.

"Would someone like to try to read any of the sentences?" Brenda asked.

Mr. Elliot kept his eyes in his lap so she wouldn't ask him.

The tall woman beside him, who had told the class she could read a little, raised a finger.

"Lorraine? Good for you."

Lorraine began to read. "I can . . . make . . . a boat. I can . . . kick — I mean, kind . . . No, it's . . . um . . ."

Mr. Elliot cringed, but no one in the class laughed. And the teacher didn't shout or wave a ruler.

"That's a hard one," Brenda said, "because this 'k' is silent. It says, 'I can knit socks.'"

Mr. Elliot went home that day with three sentences to study —

I can push a broom.
I can kick a ball.
I can play harmonica.

As he coasted home on his bike, he thought,
Maybe — just maybe — I can learn to read.

CHAPTER SEVEN

$\mathcal{T}$HE NEXT DAY Mr. Elliot pushed his broom through classrooms and hallways gathering paper scraps, stray erasers and schoolyard dirt. On one of the papers he saw the letters $b - r - o - o - m$. He almost exclaimed out loud, That's one of my words!

Mr. Elliot went into another classroom. In corners, at tables and on the sofa, pairs of children were reading to each other. As he passed one table a little girl named Sunita said, "Look, Mr. Elliot. The mice in this story are using the scraps of blue cloth from Joseph's coat to decorate their home."

Mr. Elliot did not recognize any of the words on the page. "Nice pictures," he said.

Jemma loves mice, Mr. Elliot thought. I bet she would like that book.

At his reading class that night, he asked what the word *mice* looked like. Brenda showed him *mice*, *nice*, *mouse* and *house*. She taught him ten more words besides.

Back at Jessie Lucas Public School, Mr. Elliot whistled as he pushed his broom down the hall.

"You're in a good mood today," Mr. Caracas said.

Mr. Elliot said, "Who could be in a bad mood on a beautiful day like today?"

Mr. Caracas looked out the window. "I didn't know you were so fond of rain."

Mr. Elliot just smiled because he hadn't noticed the rain and really he didn't like rainy days at all, but he couldn't tell Mr. Caracas the real reason he was happy.

As the weeks went by, the lessons got harder — and harder. Sometimes it seemed to Mr. Elliot that he'd never be able to keep straight the difference between "tr" and "th" or "cr" and "ch". He hated how "ch" in *chair* made one sound and "ch" in *school* made another. Then there was *thought* and *through* and *trough* — why did so many words have to look so much alike? And why was "gh" silent in some words, he wondered, but not in *spaghetti*?

What was the point of silent letters anyway? Why didn't whoever invented all these words just leave out the letters you couldn't hear?

One night Mr. Elliot went to Jason's hockey game, happy to forget about reading for a while. He stamped his feet when Jason stick-handled the puck out from the corner and cheered when Jason scored a goal. Later he played a crazy version of "Yankee Doodle" on his harmonica and Jemma laughed. The next day he sprinkled sand on the icy steps of Jessie Lucas Public School. The principal, Mr. Clarke, said, "Thank you, Mr. Elliot. What a thoughtful fellow you are."

My life is good, Mr. Elliot thought. Would it be such a bad thing if I didn't finish learning to read?

CHAPTER EIGHT

*T*HAT NIGHT THE SNOW blew hard and the wind whipped at the library windows. Mr. Elliot was reading quietly aloud to his teacher and making a lot of mistakes. Suddenly he banged his fist on the table. The teacher said, "You're doing fine, Graham. There are some difficult words in this piece."

As Mr. Elliot trudged home, clumpy snow stuck to his boots. Ice crystals bit his face. He balled up his cold hands in his pockets and decided, I am stupid, I cannot do it. I am too old to learn. And I am not going back to those classes.

Later that week, when Mr. Elliot went to visit his daughter and grandchildren, Jason was reading slowly to his mother. "'Come on up,' he urged. 'It wasn't hard, hon . . . honest. You won't fall. It's neat up here. Come on. Just try.'"

Enough reading, Mr. Elliot thought, and got up to leave. Then he noticed Jemma listening intently to her brother. Before long she would be learning to read too. Mr. Elliot sat down with Jemma to listen.

"'If I can do it,'" Jason read, "'you can. You're . . . taller. It's really neat up here. You've got to see it.'" Jason read slowly, and struggled with some of the words, but he kept on reading. "'You'll like it. I can't ex . . . explain it. You have to see it for yourself. Don't be such a big suck.'"

Mr. Elliot muttered, "Graham Elliot, you should be ashamed of yourself, wanting to give up so quickly."

"Pardon, Grampa?" Jemma said.

"Nothing, sweetheart. You listen to your brother."

The next week Mr. Elliot went back to his reading class at the library more determined than ever. He tried every word the teacher gave him, and even got most of them right. After class he waited till the other students had left. "Brenda," he said, "would it be possible for you to give me extra lessons?"

Brenda smiled. "I'd be happy to."

CHAPTER NINE

$\mathcal{B}$Y THE TIME the tulips poked up through the ground, Mr. Elliot could read all the words on the charts in the Grade One class. Days of the week. Months of the year. Poems about spring and popcorn, monsters and sock fluff. Lists of games — he found the words *soccer* and *baseball*. Lists of workers — he found the word *caretaker*. Mr. Elliot could read most of the words on the walls in the other classes too. Words of songs he had heard them singing. Stories the kids had written. Facts about all kinds of things — birds, inventions, thunder.

One day when Mr. Caracas was out of the school, Mr. Elliot went to the caretakers' room. He took from his mail cubby his bag of chocolate chip cookies and the form Mr. Caracas had given him so long ago.

Could he read it well enough to fill it out now? Was it too late to apply for the job of head custodian?

Name. That was easy. *Address.* He could write that now too. *How long have you worked at your present location?* None of the questions were difficult. Mr. Elliot filled out every line of the form, ate two chocolate chip cookies and went to the school secretary for an envelope and stamp. On his way home he dropped his first-ever letter in the mailbox.

He pedalled along Maple Drive and turned the corner onto Hickory Street. At Martella's Food Market he stopped to buy a can of soup for supper. Chicken Noodle. No more Cream of Spinach surprises for him!

One rainy Saturday afternoon Mr. Elliot asked his grandson, "What's that you're reading?"

"Just a book," Jason said. "But I'm stuck on this word."

"Learning to read is hard work," Mr. Elliot said. He unplugged the steaming kettle. "I know because I've been learning too."

Jason laughed. "Grownups don't have to learn to read. They can read already."

"Some of us are just good at pretending," Mr. Elliot said. "But I've been doing my best to learn, so I won't have to pretend anymore." He stirred his coffee as Jason stared at him, wide-eyed. "Seeing you try so hard with your reading helped give me the courage to keep trying."

"Really?"

"Really. That and your little sister's big brown eyes. Now, let's have a look at that word."

CHAPTER TEN

ONE SPRING DAY, after all the kids had gone home from school and the teachers were all at a meeting, Mr. Elliot was sweeping in the Grade Five classroom. The book he'd seen the teacher reading to her class recently was propped on the chalk ledge. *Angel Square* it was called.

Mr. Elliot picked it up and ran his hand over the cover. He flipped through the pages. There were a lot of words on every page. But Mr. Elliot wanted to know who beat up Sammy's father in the streetcar barns. He was sure if he took his time, he could read the book and find out. He would ask the teacher tomorrow if he could borrow it.

Later, in the Grade Two classroom, Mr. Elliot was moving a table so he could sweep under it. A few books fell to the floor and one of them opened. In the book's pictures, there were mice and bits of blue cloth — the same mice and bits of blue cloth that Sunita had shown him all those months ago.

Mr. Elliot picked up the book. He turned to the first page. There were not too many words in this book, and no one was around, so he sat down on the small chair by the small table in the empty classroom and began to read.

Why! This story isn't about the mice at all, Mr. Elliot realized. It's about a boy and his grandfather. The story of the mice is only in the pictures. I bet both Jemma and Jason would like this story.

Mr. Elliot continued to read the words and the pictures. When he came to the part where the boy makes a story, Mr. Elliot smiled. When he saw that the mouse had made a story too, he laughed out loud.

"Why, Mr. Elliot," the teacher said, "what are you doing?"

"I'm sorry," he said, quickly putting the book back on the table and picking up his broom. "I didn't see you come in. I was just . . . I thought maybe . . ." But he didn't feel ashamed — not like he used to, when he was afraid someone would find out he couldn't read.

"I've been taking some classes, Mrs. Evans," he said. "Reading classes. I've learned now. To read. Finally I've learned."

"Oh!" Mrs. Evans said.

"I used to be afraid of reading, but I have these grandchildren, Jemma kept asking me to read her a story, and Mr. Caracas wanted me to apply for his job and . . ." Mr. Elliot laughed at how the words were gushing out of him like sudsy water out of a bucket.

"Mr. Elliot, that's a wonderful story," Mrs. Evans said. "The children here at Jessie Lucas would love it. I could help you write it, if you'd like."

"I'm not much of a writer yet, but you've given me an idea. By the way, could I take this book home, just for one night?"

"Certainly. Keep it till next week if you'd like. And Mr. Elliot? Please borrow another book from our classroom any time you'd like."

CHAPTER ELEVEN

MR. ELLIOT SAT in the big comfy chair in his daughter's living room. He watched Jemma crawling around the floor, pushing her bus full of little people around the legs of the tables.

"Time to get ready for bed," her mother said.

Jemma pushed the bus down the hall to her room. In her red pyjamas she brought her grandfather his harmonica and climbed into his lap.

Mr. Elliot set the harmonica on the table beside them and picked up the book Mrs. Evans had let him borrow. "First, little Jemma, I've got something I'd like to show you."

"I'm not little," Jemma said. "I'm big now."

Mr. Elliot laughed. "Me too!" His grandson came into the living room, munching an apple.

"Jason, you might enjoy this too."

With a grandchild snuggled in on each side of him, Mr. Elliot ran his hand over the cover of the book. He took a deep breath and read, *"Something From Nothing."* He started to read the author's name, but he'd never seen it before and didn't know if the "Ph" at the beginning was a "p" sound or an "f" sound. And were those "e"s supposed to be silent?

"By Somebody Gilman," Mr. Elliot said and opened the book to the first page.

"When Joseph was a baby, his grandfather made him a wonderful blanket . . ."

Each time Mr. Elliot turned the page, Jemma shivered or laughed. When he had finished reading the book, Jason said, "I'm going to go write a story too. Just like Joseph."

"When you've done that," Mr. Elliot said, "I have another project I'd like you to help me with, okay?"

Jemma slapped the book in Mr. Elliot's lap. "Read me this again, Grampa."

As Mr. Elliot read the story again, Jemma's thumb slid into her mouth. When he closed the book, she reached over to the table beside her. She picked up Mr. Elliot's harmonica and stuck it into his hand.

Mr. Elliot smiled. Before playing *Hush Little Baby*, he warmed up with a slow rendition of *I'm the King of the Ca-a-stle.*

Chapter Twelve

ONE HOT DAY, not long before summer holidays, Mr. Elliot hoisted the flag in front of Jessie Lucas Public School as proud as could be. He winked at Derek, who was again outside the principal's office. "I hope you're not in too much trouble to come to the assembly this morning," he whispered.

"I'm not in trouble," Derek said. "I have an appointment with Mr. Clarke. I'm going to read him this book. I can read it myself now."

"Good for you, Derek. That's great."

After recess everyone filed into the gym for the end-of-the-year assembly. Mr. Elliot was pleased to see Derek coming in with his class, and Mario and Sunita. He especially wanted them to be there for what he was going to do.

In front of the gym packed with kids, the junior choir sang "Land of the Silver Birch" and the senior choir sang "Climb Every Mountain." Next, a boy gave his prize-winning speech about the freedom to read. Mr. Elliot could not imagine anyone wanting to stop someone from reading. The drama club did a play about summer safety, the gym teacher handed out athletic awards, and the principal made a speech. At the end he thanked Mr. Caracas for all the hard work he had done and gave him a present for his retirement.

Mr. Caracas thanked everyone and said, "I'm pleased to announce that the new head caretaker when you come back to school in the fall will be . . . Mr. Elliot."

Mr. Elliot went to the stage. "I'm very happy. I hope I will do as good a job as Mr. Caracas." He shuffled his feet and swallowed. "I want to end the assembly," he said, "by reading something I have written — with the help of my grandson, Jason." He wiped the sweat from his forehead. "Mrs. Evans helped a little too."

The principal cleared his throat and looked at his watch. He hadn't been expecting this. But Mrs. Evans and Jason stood and led the school in a big round of applause, so Mr. Clarke sat down with everyone else to listen.

When all was quiet, Mr. Elliot began to read, loudly and slowly and proudly:

> *Mr. Elliot liked being a caretaker.*
> *And he liked being a grandfather.*
> *But Mr. Elliot had a problem . . .*

When Mr. Elliot finished the part about reading to his grandchildren and playing *King of the Castle* on his harmonica, everyone in the gym clapped and cheered.

Mr. Clarke walked to the stage, his hand raised. The crowd hushed. "When we come back to Jessie Lucas in the fall," Mr. Clarke announced, "we will have a big party to celebrate what Mr. Elliot has done."

"It can be a reading party," said Mrs. Evans.

Derek said, "We can all dress up as our favourite book characters."

"The party for my grandfather," Jason said, "will be a party fit for a king."

ACKNOWLEDGEMENTS

Elijah Allen, to whom this book is dedicated, is head custodian at Sir Alexander Mackenzie School in Inuvik. Of learning to read as an adult he has said, "It is like I have been climbing a steep hill all my life and now I can see the valley on the other side." Elijah Allen has served on the Northwest Territories Literacy Council and still enjoys speaking to children and adults in many Northern communities about his experiences. His greatest pleasure now that he can read is being able to read his Bible himself instead of listening to its stories on tape.

Jessie Lucas, after whom Mr. Elliot's school is named, was crucial to the success of Frontier College, a volunteer-based Canadian literacy organization founded in 1899. Jessie Lucas worked closely with the founder of the college and its teachers from 1920 to 1964. She died in 1996 at the age of 102.

Reference: Page 44

Angel Square by Brian Doyle. Published by Groundwood Books, 1984.

About the Author

KATHY STINSON sorted mail, taught school, and waited tables before figuring out, while at home with her two chidren, that what she really wanted to do was write. Many of her books have been released in Germany, England, Sweden, Denmark, Finland, Japan, Holland, Poland, Venezuela or China, as well as Canada and the United States. When she is not busy writing, she likes to read other people's books, do jigsaw puzzles, work in her garden, and go for walks in the woods near her home in Ontario.

ABOUT THE ILLUSTRATOR

KASIA CHARKO has illustrated many children's picture books and young adult novels, including *A Riddle of Roses*, *The Princess Who Danced With Cranes*, *From Poppa* and *The Boogie Woogie Bear*. She loves to make words come alive for children with her paintings. She started doing illustrations when she lived in England, and has since done all kinds: from editorial to advertising. She currently lives with her family in Ontario, and enjoys going hiking with her dogs.